FURTHER ADVENTURES
OF
PETER RABBIT

This Book Belongs to:

Chantel
McCabe

FURTHER ADVENTURES
OF
PETER RABBIT

by BEATRIX POTTER
With Her Original Illustrations

The Tale of the Flopsy Bunnies
The Tale of Mrs. Tittlemouse ● *The Tale of Timmy Tiptoes*
The Tale of Mr. Tod ● *The Tale of Pigling Bland*
Ginger and Pickles

Derrydale Books ● New York

This volume contains the complete and unabridged texts of the original editions. They have been completely reset for this volume.

This 1989 edition is published by Derrydale Books, distributed by Crown Publishers, Inc., 225 Park Avenue South, New York, New York 10003.

Printed and bound in the United States of America

Library of Congress Cataloging-in-Publication Data
Potter, Beatrix, 1866–1943.
Further adventures of Peter Rabbit : six stories of Peter Rabbit and his friends by Beatrix Potter, with her original illustrations.
p.   cm.
Contents: The tale of the Flopsy bunnies—The tale of Mrs. Tittlemouse—The tale of Timmy Tiptoes—The tale of Mr. Tod—The tale of Pigling Bland—Ginger and Pickles.
ISBN 0-517-68371-7
1. Children's stories, English. [1. Animals—Fiction. 2. Short stories.] I. Title.
PZ7.P85Fu 1989
[E]—dc20   89-33689   CIP   AC
h g f e d c b a
Book design by Jean Krulis

CONTENTS

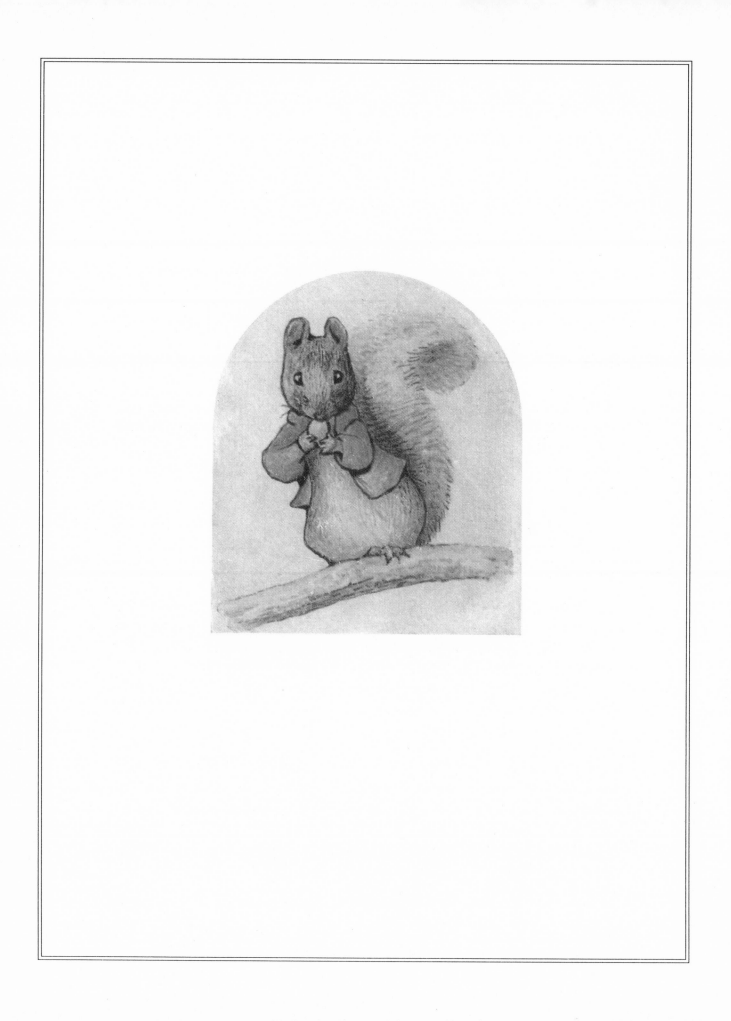

FOREWORD

The name Beatrix Potter conjures up a miniature world, lovingly rendered in all its tiniest details, so complete, so warm and intimate, that we can easily dream ourselves into it. We return to a time when each day is a new adventure, when the novel uniqueness of everyday things is cherished and transformed into the stuff of fantasy.

In *The Tale of Mrs. Tittlemouse*, children delight in the home of the woodmouse with its "yards and yards of sandy passages." Old and young alike are caught up in the houseproud mouse's struggles with a variety of unwelcome insect and amphibian visitors. But the young child, struggling to create order in his knowledge of the world, identifies both with Thomasina Tittlemouse, who tries to maintain the spotlessness of her home, as well as with the unlicensed intruders, who give in to their impulses. The genius of Beatrix Potter is that through this very gentle story she still speaks, with no sense of talking down, to the basic concerns of the child.

In *The Tale of the Flopsy Bunnies*, we come upon the six sleeping bunnies nestled trustingly around a lettuce and exposed with the vulnerability and innocence of infants. Put into a sack by the farmer, Mr. McGregor, these nephews and nieces of Peter Rabbit dream that their mother is "turning them over in bed." After the bunnies are rescued, we join them, sharing their childlike need to see how it will all come out, as they follow Mr. McGregor. Beatrix Potter painted these hidden witnesses, in poses of alert listening, with a gentle irony, all the more powerful for not showing much of the humans involved. We are made aware of the secret watchfulness of nature, that other world with motives and concerns of its own, unseen by self-involved humans.

These are tender stories, yet they are often about struggles. Within the songlike simplicity of *The Tale of Timmy Tiptoes*, we are told of Timmy Tiptoes's encounter with a gang of squirrels angry because they mistakenly think that he has stolen their nuts. In another story, Pigling Bland sets off on his adventures like the hero of a fairy tale, and indeed, rescues a damsel in distress. And in *The Tale of Mr. Tod*, we watch with suspense the feared fox concoct an ingenious contraption of buckets and water to outwit the badger who has usurped his home. During this contest, Peter Rabbit and Benjamin Bunny wait in a tunnel under the house to rescue Flopsy's bunnies, kidnapped by the badger.

It is fitting that we end this treasury with *Ginger and Pickles*, which pokes gentle fun at that hub of English village life, the general store, for we recognize in many of the customers old friends—Peter Rabbit, Squirrel Nutkin, Jemima Puddle-duck, and others. Indeed, it was the old-fashioned and down-to-earth village and farming life of the green, gently hilly country of England's Lake District that Beatrix Potter loved. But she was born far from this life, in 1866, into the loneliness of the third-floor nursery of a stultifyingly well-regulated middle-class London home. As she never was given the opportunity to make friends, it was the family's summer holidays to Scotland that gave Beatrix and her younger brother their first taste of freedom. She and her brother captured and drew animals, noting their habits. But it was her need to reach out that brought the Peter Rabbit books into being. The first little book started life as an illustrated letter to the five-year-old son of her former governess. The letter was later published as a book in 1901, and as following books created more success, Beatrix was able, at the age of thirty-nine, to buy a farm in her beloved Lake District. Thus it was that in being true to her own inner vision, born in solitude, she eventually was able to take strides into the world she cherished. She left behind a legacy of little tales that can be reread countless times. They will always be treasured for their beauty, vitality, and integrity.

ELLEN S. SHAPIRO

Brooklyn, New York
1989

THE TALE OF
THE FLOPSY BUNNIES

For All Little Friends of
Mr. McGregor and Peter and Benjamin

It is said that the effect of eating too much lettuce is "soporific."

I have never felt sleepy after eating lettuces; but then I am not a rabbit.

They certainly had a very soporific effect upon the Flopsy Bunnies!

When Benjamin Bunny grew up, he married his Cousin Flopsy. They had a large family, and they were very improvident and cheerful.

I do not remember the separate names of their children; they were generally called the "Flopsy Bunnies."

As there was not always quite enough to eat,—Benjamin used to borrow cabbages from Flopsy's brother, Peter Rabbit, who kept a nursery garden.

Sometimes Peter Rabbit had no cabbages to spare.

When this happened, the Flopsy Bunnies went across the field to a rubbish heap, in the ditch outside Mr. McGregor's garden.

Mr. McGregor's rubbish heap was a mixture. There were jam pots and paper bags, and mountains of chopped grass from the mowing machine (which always tasted oily), and some rotten vegetable marrows and an old boot or two. One day—oh joy!—there were a quantity of overgrown lettuces, which had "shot" into flower.

The Flopsy Bunnies simply stuffed lettuces. By degrees, one after another, they were overcome with slumber, and lay down in the mown grass.

Benjamin was not so much overcome as his children. Before going to sleep he was sufficiently wide awake to put a paper bag over his head to keep off the flies.

The little Flopsy Bunnies slept delightfully in the warm sun. From the lawn beyond the garden came the distant clacketty sound of the mowing machine. The blue-bottles buzzed about the wall, and a little old mouse picked over the rubbish among the jam pots.

(I can tell you her name, she was called Thomasina Tittle-mouse, a woodmouse with a long tail.)

She rustled across the paper bag, and awakened Benjamin Bunny.

The mouse apologized profusely, and said that she knew Peter Rabbit.

While she and Benjamin were talking, close under the wall, they heard a heavy tread above their heads; and suddenly Mr. Mc-Gregor emptied out a sackful of lawn mowings right upon the top of the sleeping Flopsy Bunnies! Benjamin shrank down under his paper bag. The mouse hid in a jam pot.

The little rabbits smiled sweetly in their sleep under the shower of grass; they did not awake because the lettuces had been so soporific.

They dreamt that their mother Flopsy was tucking them up in a hay bed.

Mr. McGregor looked down after emptying his sack. He saw some funny little brown tips of ears sticking up through the lawn mowings. He stared at them for some time.

Presently a fly settled on one of them and it moved.

Mr. McGregor climbed down on to the rubbish heap—

"One, two, three, four! five! six leetle rabbits!" said he as he dropped them into his sack. The Flopsy Bunnies dreamt that their mother was turning them over in bed. They stirred a little in their sleep, but still they did not wake up.

Mr. McGregor tied up the sack and left it on the wall.

He went to put away the mowing machine.

While he was gone, Mrs. Flopsy Bunny (who had remained at home) came across the field.

She looked suspiciously at the sack and wondered where everybody was?

Then the mouse came out of her jam pot, and Benjamin took the paper bag off his head, and they told the doleful tale.

Benjamin and Flopsy were in despair, they could not undo the string.

But Mrs. Tittlemouse was a resourceful person. She nibbled a hole in the bottom corner of the sack.

The little rabbits were pulled out and pinched to wake them.

Their parents stuffed the empty sack with three rotten vegetable marrows, an old blackingbrush and two decayed turnips.

Then they all hid under a bush and watched for Mr. McGregor.

Mr. McGregor came back and picked up the sack, and carried it off.

He carried it hanging down, as if it were rather heavy.

The Flopsy Bunnies followed at a safe distance.

They watched him go into his house.

And then they crept up to the window to listen.

Mr. McGregor threw down the sack on the stone floor in a way that would have been extremely painful to the Flopsy Bunnies, if they had happened to have been inside it.

They could hear him drag his chair on the flags, and chuckle—

"One, two, three, four, five, six leetle rabbits!" said Mr. McGregor.

"Eh? What's that? What have they been spoiling now?" enquired Mrs. McGregor.

"One, two, three, four, five, six leetle fat rabbits!" repeated Mr. McGregor, counting on his fingers —"one, two, three—"

"Don't you be silly: what do you mean, you silly old man?"

"In the sack! one, two, three, four, five, six!" replied Mr. McGregor.

(The youngest Flopsy Bunny got upon the windowsill.)

Mrs. McGregor took hold of the sack and felt it. She said she could feel six, but they must be *old* rabbits, because they were so hard and all different shapes.

"Not fit to eat; but the skins will do fine to line my old cloak."

"Line your old cloak?" shouted Mr. McGregor—"I shall sell them and buy myself baccy!"

"Rabbit tobacco! I shall skin them and cut off their heads."

Mrs. McGregor untied the sack and put her hand inside.

When she felt the vegetables she became very very angry. She said that Mr. McGregor had "done it a purpose."

And Mr. McGregor was very angry too. One of the rotten marrows came flying through the kitchen window, and hit the youngest Flopsy Bunny.

It was rather hurt.

Then Benjamin and Flopsy thought that it was time to go home.

So Mr. McGregor did not get his tobacco, and Mrs. McGregor did not get her rabbit skins.

But next Christmas Thomasina Tittlemouse got a present of enough rabbit wool to make herself a cloak and a hood, and a handsome muff and a pair of warm mittens.

THE TALE OF
MRS.
TITTLEMOUSE

Nellie's
Little Book

Once upon a time there was a woodmouse, and her name was Mrs. Tittlemouse.

She lived in a bank under a hedge.

Such a funny house! There were yards and yards of sandy passages, leading to store-rooms and nut cellars and seed cellars, all amongst the roots of the hedge.

There was a kitchen, a parlor, a pantry, and a larder.

Also, there was Mrs. Tittlemouse's bedroom, where she slept in a little box bed!

Mrs. Tittlemouse was a most terribly tidy particular little mouse, always sweeping and dusting the soft sandy floors.

Sometimes a beetle lost its way in the passages.

"Shuh! shuh! little dirty feet!" said Mrs. Tittlemouse, clattering her dustpan.

And one day a little old woman ran up and down in a red spotty cloak.

"Your house is on fire, Mother Ladybird! Fly away home to your children!"

Another day, a big fat spider came in to shelter from the rain.

"Beg pardon, is this not Miss Muffet's?"

"Go away, you bold bad spider! Leaving ends of cobweb all over my nice clean house!"

She bundled the spider out at a window.

He let himself down the hedge with a long thin bit of string.

Mrs. Tittlemouse went on her way to a distant storeroom, to fetch cherrystones and thistle-down seed for dinner.

All along the passage she sniffed, and looked at the floor.

"I smell a smell of honey; is it the cowslips outside, in the hedge? I am sure I can see the marks of little dirty feet."

Suddenly round a corner, she met Babbitty Bumble—"Zizz, Bizz, Bizzz!" said the bumble bee.

Mrs. Tittlemouse looked at her severely. She wished that she had a broom.

"Good-day, Babbitty Bumble; I should be glad to buy some bees-wax. But what are you doing down here? Why do you always come in at a window, and say, Zizz, Bizz, Bizzz?" Mrs. Tittlemouse began to get cross.

"Zizz, Wizz, Wizzz!" replied Babbitty Bumble in a peevish squeak. She sidled down a passage, and disappeared into a storeroom which had been used for acorns.

Mrs. Tittlemouse had eaten the acorns before Christmas; the storeroom ought to have been empty.

But it was full of untidy dry moss.

Mrs. Tittlemouse began to pull out the moss. Three or four other bees put their heads out, and buzzed fiercely.

"I am not in the habit of letting lodgings; this is an intrusion!" said Mrs. Tittlemouse. "I will have them turned out —" "Buzz! Buzz! Buzzz!"—"I wonder who would help me?" "Bizz, Wizz, Wizzz!"

—"I will not have Mr. Jackson; he never wipes his feet."

Mrs. Tittlemouse decided to leave the bees till after dinner.

When she got back to the parlor, she heard some one coughing in a fat voice; and there sat Mr. Jackson himself!

He was sitting all over a small rocking chair, twiddling his thumbs and smiling, with his feet on the fender.

He lived in a drain below the hedge, in a very dirty wet ditch.

"How do you do, Mr. Jackson? Deary me, you have got very wet!"

"Thank you, thank you, thank you, Mrs. Tittlemouse! I'll sit awhile and dry myself," said Mr. Jackson.

He sat and smiled, and the water dripped off his coat tails. Mrs. Tittlemouse went round with a mop.

He sat such a while that he had to be asked if he would take some dinner?

First she offered him cherry-stones. "Thank you, thank you, Mrs. Tittlemouse! No teeth, no teeth, no teeth!" said Mr. Jackson.

He opened his mouth most unnecessarily wide; he certainly had not a tooth in his head.

Then she offered him thistle-down seed—"Tiddly, widdly, widdly! Pouff, pouff, puff!" said Mr. Jackson. He blew the thistle-down all over the room.

"Thank you, thank you, thank you, Mrs. Tittlemouse! Now what I really—*really* should like—would be a little dish of honey!"

"I am afraid I have not got any, Mr. Jackson!" said Mrs. Tittlemouse.

"Tiddly, widdly, widdly, Mrs. Tittlemouse!" said the smiling Mr. Jackson, "I can *smell* it; that is why I came to call."

Mr. Jackson rose ponderously from the table, and began to look into the cupboards.

Mrs. Tittlemouse followed him with a dishcloth, to wipe his large wet footmarks off the parlor floor.

When he had convinced himself that there was no honey in the cupboards, he began to walk down the passage.

"Indeed, indeed, you will stick fast, Mr. Jackson!"

"Tiddly, widdly, widdly, Mrs. Tittlemouse!"

First he squeezed into the pantry.

"Tiddly, widdly, widdly? No honey? No honey, Mrs. Tittlemouse?"

There were three creepy-crawly people hiding in the plate rack. Two of them got away; but the littlest one he caught.

Then he squeezed into the larder. Miss Butterfly was tasting the sugar; but she flew away out of the window.

"Tiddly, widdly, widdly, Mrs. Tittlemouse; you seem to have plenty of visitors!"

"And without any invitation!" said Mrs. Thomasina Tittlemouse.

They went along the sandy passage—"Tiddly, widdly—" "Buzz! Wizz! Wizz!"

He met Babbitty round a corner, and snapped her up, and put her down again.

"I do not like bumble bees. They are all over bristles," said Mr. Jackson, wiping his mouth with his coat sleeve.

"Get out, you nasty old toad!" shrieked Babbitty Bumble.

"I shall go distracted!" scolded Mrs. Tittlemouse.

She shut herself up in the nut cellar while Mr. Jackson pulled out the bees-nest. He seemed to have no objection to stings.

When Mrs. Tittlemouse ventured to come out—everybody had gone away.

But the untidiness was something dreadful—"Never did I see such a mess—smears of honey; and moss, and thistledown—and marks of big and little dirty feet—all over my nice clean house!"

She gathered up the moss and the remains of the bees-wax.

Then she went out and fetched some twigs, to partly close up the front door.

"I will make it too small for Mr. Jackson!"

She fetched soft soap, and flannel, and a new scrubbing brush from the storeroom. But she was too tired to do any more. First she fell asleep in her chair, and then she went to bed.

"Will it ever be tidy again?" said poor Mrs. Tittlemouse.

Next morning she got up very early and began a spring cleaning which lasted a fortnight.

She swept, and scrubbed, and dusted; and she rubbed up the furniture with beeswax, and polished her little tin spoons.

When it was all beautifully neat and clean, she gave a party to five other little mice, without Mr. Jackson.

He smelt the party and came up the bank, but he could not squeeze in at the door.

So they handed him out acorn cupfuls of honeydew through the window, and he was not at all offended.

He sat outside in the sun, and said—"Tiddly, widdly, widdly! Your very good health, Mrs. Tittlemouse!"

THE TALE OF
TIMMY
TIPTOES

For Many Unknown Little Friends,
Including Monica

Once upon a time there was a little fat comfortable grey squirrel, called Timmy Tiptoes. He had a nest thatched with leaves in the top of a tall tree; and he had a little squirrel wife called Goody.

Timmy Tiptoes sat out, enjoying the breeze; he whisked his tail and chuckled—"Little wife Goody, the nuts are ripe; we must lay up a store for winter and spring." Goody Tiptoes was busy pushing moss under the thatch—"The nest is so snug, we shall be sound asleep all winter." "Then we shall wake up all the thinner, when there is nothing to eat in spring-time," replied prudent Timothy.

When Timmy and Goody Tiptoes came to the nut thicket, they found other squirrels were there already.

Timmy took off his jacket and hung it on a twig; they worked away quietly by themselves.

Every day they made several journeys and picked quantities of nuts. They carried them away in bags, and stored them in several hollow stumps near the tree where they had built their nest.

When these stumps were full, they began to empty the bags into a hole high up a tree, that had belonged to a woodpecker; the nuts rattled down—down—down inside.

"How shall you ever get them out again? It is like a money box!" said Goody.

"I shall be much thinner before springtime, my love," said Timmy Tiptoes, peeping into the hole.

They did collect quantities—because they did not lose them! Squirrels who bury their nuts in the ground lose more than half, because they cannot remember the place.

The most forgetful squirrel in the wood was called Silvertail. He began to dig, and he could not remember. And then he dug again and found some nuts that did not belong to him; and there was a fight. And other squirrels began to dig,—the whole wood was in commotion!

Unfortunately, just at this time a flock of little birds flew by, from bush to bush, searching for green caterpillars and spiders. There were several sorts of little birds, twittering different songs.

The first one sang—"Who's bin digging-up *my* nuts? Who's-been-digging-up *my* nuts?"

And another sang—"Little bita bread and-*no*-cheese! Little bit-a-bread an'-*no*-cheese!"

The squirrels followed and listened. The first little bird flew into the bush where Timmy and Goody Tiptoes were quietly tying up their bags, and it sang—"Who's-bin digging-up *my* nuts? Who's been digging-up *my*-nuts?"

Timmy Tiptoes went on with his work without replying; indeed, the little bird did not expect an answer. It was only singing its natural song, and it meant nothing at all.

But when the other squirrels heard that song, they rushed upon Timmy Tiptoes and cuffed and scratched him, and upset his bag of nuts. The innocent little bird which had caused all the mischief, flew away in a fright!

Timmy rolled over and over, and then turned tail and fled towards his nest, followed by a crowd of squirrels shouting—"Who's-been digging-up *my*-nuts?"

They caught him and dragged him up the very same tree, where there was the little round hole, and they pushed him in. The hole was much too small for Timmy Tiptoes' figure. They squeezed him dreadfully, it was a wonder they did not break his ribs. "We will leave him here till he confesses," said Silvertail Squirrel and he shouted into the hole—"Who's-been-digging-up *my*-nuts?"

Timmy Tiptoes made no reply; he had tumbled down inside the tree, upon half a peck of nuts belonging to himself. He lay quite stunned and still.

Goody Tiptoes picked up the nut bags and went home. She made a cup of tea for Timmy; but he didn't come and didn't come.

Goody Tiptoes passed a lonely and unhappy night. Next morning she ventured back to the nut bushes to look for him; but the other unkind squirrels drove her away.

She wandered all over the wood, calling—

"Timmy Tiptoes! Timmy Tiptoes! Oh, where is Timmy Tiptoes?"

In the meantime Timmy Tiptoes came to his senses. He found
himself tucked up in a little moss
bed, very much in the dark, feeling sore; it seemed to be under
ground. Timmy coughed and
groaned, because his ribs hurted
him. There was a chirpy noise,
and a small striped Chipmunk ap-
peared with a night light, and
hoped he felt better?

It was most kind to Timmy Tiptoes; it lent him its nightcap; and
the house was full of provisions.

The Chipmunk explained that it
had rained nuts through the top of
the tree—"Besides, I found a few
buried!" It laughed and chuckled
when it heard Timmy's story.
While Timmy was confined to
bed, it 'ticed him to eat quantities
—"But how shall I ever get out
through that hole unless I thin
myself? My wife will be anxious!"
"Just another nut—or two nuts;
let me crack them for you," said
the Chipmunk. Timmy Tiptoes
grew fatter and fatter!

Now Goody Tiptoes had set to work again by herself. She did not put any more nuts into the woodpecker's hole, because she had always doubted how they could be got out again. She hid them under a tree root; they rattled down, down, down. Once when Goody emptied an extra big bagful, there was a decided squeak; and next time Goody brought another bagful, a little striped Chipmunk scrambled out in a hurry.

"It is getting perfectly full-up downstairs; the sitting room is full, and they are rolling along the passage; and my husband, Chippy Hackee, has run away and left me. What is the explanation of these showers of nuts?"

"I am sure I beg your pardon; I did not know that anybody lived here," said Mrs. Goody Tiptoes; "but where is Chippy Hackee? My husband, Timmy Tiptoes, has run away too." "I know where Chippy is; a little bird told me," said Mrs. Chippy Hackee.

She led the way to the wood-pecker's tree, and they listened at the hole.

Down below there was a noise of nutcrackers, and a fat squirrel voice and a thin squirrel voice were singing together—

"My little old man and I fell out,
   How shall we bring this matter about?
   Bring it about as well as you can,
   And get you gone, you little old man!"

"You could squeeze in, through that little round hole," said Goody Tiptoes. "Yes, I could," said the Chipmunk, "but my husband, Chippy Hackee, bites!"

Down below there was a noise of cracking nuts and nibbling; and then the fat squirrel voice and the thin squirrel voice sang—

"For the diddlum day
   Day diddle dum di!
   Day diddle diddle dum day!"

Then Goody peeped in at the hole, and called down—"Timmy Tiptoes! Oh fie, Timmy Tiptoes!" And Timmy replied, "Is that you, Goody Tiptoes? Why, certainly!"

He came up and kissed Goody through the hole; but he was so fat that he could not get out.

Chippy Hackee was not too fat, but he did not want to come; he stayed down below and chuckled.

And so it went on for a fortnight; till a big wind blew off the top of the tree, and opened up the hole and let in the rain.

Then Timmy Tiptoes came out, and went home with an umbrella.

But Chippy Hackee contin-
ued to camp out for another
week, although it was uncomfortable.

At last a large bear came
walking through the wood.
Perhaps he also was looking
for nuts; he seemed to be sniff-
ing around.

Chippy Hackee went home in a hurry!

And when Chippy Hackee got home, he found he had caught a cold in his head; and he was more uncomfortable still.

And now Timmy and Goody Tiptoes keep their nut store fastened up with a little padlock.

And whenever that little bird sees the Chipmunks, he sings — "Who's-been-digging-up *my*-nuts? Who's been digging-up *my*-nuts?" But nobody ever answers!

THE TALE OF
MR. TOD

For William Francis of Ulva—Someday!

I have made many books about well-behaved people. Now, for a change, I am going to make a story about two disagreeable people, called Tommy Brock and Mr. Tod.

Nobody could call Mr. Tod "nice." The rabbits could not bear him; they could smell him half a mile off. He was of a wandering habit and he had foxy whiskers; they never knew where he would be next.

One day he was living in a stick-house in the coppice [grove], causing terror to the family of old Mr. Benjamin Bouncer. Next day he

moved into a pollard willow near the lake, frightening the wild ducks and the water rats.

In winter and early spring he might generally be found in an earth amongst the rocks at the top of Bull Banks, under Oatmeal Crag.

He had half a dozen houses, but he was seldom at home.

The houses were not always empty when Mr. Tod moved *out*; because sometimes Tommy Brock moved *in*; (without asking leave).

Tommy Brock was a short bristly fat waddling person with a grin; he grinned all over his face. He was not nice in his habits. He ate wasp nests and frogs and worms; and he waddled about by moonlight, digging things up.

His clothes were very dirty; and as he slept in the daytime, he aloutside the burrow, in a muffler; smoking a pipe of rabbit tobacco.

He lived with his son Benjamin Bunny and his daughter-in-law Flopsy, who had a young family. Old Mr. Bouncer was in charge of the family that afternoon, because Benjamin and Flopsy had gone out.

ways went to bed in his boots. And the bed which he went to bed in was generally Mr. Tod's.

Now Tommy Brock did occasionally eat rabbit pie; but it was only very little young ones occasionally, when other food was really scarce. He was friendly with old Mr. Bouncer; they agreed in disliking the wicked otters and Mr. Tod; they often talked over that painful subject.

Old Mr. Bouncer was stricken in years. He sat in the spring sunshine

The little rabbit babies were just old enough to open their blue eyes and kick. They lay in a fluffy bed of rabbit wool and hay, in a shallow burrow, separate from the main rabbit hole. To tell the truth—old Mr. Bouncer had forgotten them.

He sat in the sun, and conversed cordially with Tommy Brock, who was passing through the wood with a sack and a little spud which he used for digging, and some mole traps. He complained bitterly about the scarcity of pheasants'

eggs, and accused Mr. Tod of poaching them. And the otters had cleared off all the frogs while he was asleep in winter—"I have not had a good square meal for a fortnight, I am living on pig-nuts. I shall have to turn vegetarian and eat my own tail!" said Tommy Brock.

It was not much of a joke, but it tickled old Mr. Bouncer; because Tommy Brock was so fat and stumpy and grinning.

So old Mr. Bouncer laughed; and pressed Tommy Brock to come inside, to taste a slice of seed cake and "a glass of my daughter Flopsy's cowslip wine." Tommy Brock squeezed himself into the rabbit hole with alacrity.

Then old Mr. Bouncer smoked another pipe, and gave Tommy Brock a cabbage leaf cigar which was so very strong that it made Tommy Brock grin more than ever; and the smoke filled the burrow. Old Mr. Bouncer coughed and laughed; and Tommy Brock puffed and grinned.

And Mr. Bouncer laughed and coughed, and shut his eyes because of the cabbage smoke . . . .

When Flopsy and Benjamin came back old Mr. Bouncer woke up. Tommy Brock and all the young rabbit babies had disappeared!

Mr. Bouncer would not confess that he had admitted anybody into the rabbit hole. But the smell of badger was undeniable; and there were round heavy footmarks in the sand. He was in disgrace; Flopsy wrung her ears, and slapped him.

Benjamin Bunny set off at once after Tommy Brock.

There was not much difficulty in tracking him; he had left his footmark and gone slowly up the wind-

The path led to a part of the thicket where the trees had been cleared; there were leafy oak stumps, and a sea of blue hyacinths—but the smell that made Benjamin stop was *not* the smell of flowers!

Mr. Tod's stick house was before him; and, for once, Mr. Tod was at home. There was not only a foxy flavor in proof of it—there was smoke coming out of the broken pail that served as a chimney.

ing footpath through the wood. Here he had rooted up the moss and wood sorrel. There he had dug quite a deep hole for dog darnel; and had set a mole trap. A little stream crossed the way. Benjamin skipped lightly over dry-foot; the badger's heavy steps showed plainly in the mud.

Benjamin Bunny sat up, staring; his whiskers twitched. Inside the stick house somebody dropped a plate, and said something. Benjamin stamped his foot, and bolted.

He never stopped till he came to the other side of the wood. Apparently Tommy Brock had turned the same way. Upon the top of the wall there were again the marks of badger; and some ravellings of a sack had caught on a briar.

Benjamin climbed over the wall, into a meadow. He found another mole trap newly set; he was still upon the track of Tommy Brock. It was getting late in the afternoon. Other rabbits were coming out to enjoy the evening air. One of them in a blue coat, by himself, was busily hunting for dandelions.— "Cousin Peter! Peter Rabbit, Peter Rabbit!" shouted Benjamin Bunny.

The blue coated rabbit sat up with pricked ears—"Whatever is the matter, Cousin Benjamin? Is it a cat? or John Stoat Ferret?"

"No, no, no! He's bagged my family—Tommy Brock—in a sack —have you seen him?"

"Tommy Brock? how many, Cousin Benjamin?"

"Seven, Cousin Peter, and all of them twins! Did he come this way? Please tell me quick!"

"Yes, yes; not ten minutes since . . . . he said they were *caterpillars*; I did think they were kicking rather hard, for caterpillars."

"Which way? which way has he gone, Cousin Peter?"

"He had a sack with something 'live in it; I watched him set a mole trap. Let me use my mind, Cousin Benjamin; tell me from the beginning," Benjamin did so.

"My Uncle Bouncer has displayed a lamentable want of discretion for his years;" said Peter reflectively, "but there are two hopeful circumstances. Your family is alive and kicking; and Tommy Brock has had refreshments. He will probably go to sleep, and keep them for breakfast." "Which way?" "Cousin Benjamin, compose yourself. I know very well which way. Because Mr.

Tod was at home in the stick house he has gone to Mr. Tod's other house, at the top of Bull Banks. I partly know, because he offered to leave any message at Sister Cottontail's; he said he would be passing." (Cottontail had married a black rabbit, and gone to live on the hill.)

Peter hid his dandelions, and accompanied the afflicted parent, who was all of atwitter. They crossed several fields and began to climb the hill; the tracks of Tommy Brock were plainly to be seen. He seemed to have put down the sack every dozen yards, to rest.

"He must be very puffed; we are close behind him, by the scent. What a nasty person!" said Peter.

The sunshine was still warm and slanting on the hill pastures. Half way up, Cottontail was sitting in her doorway, with four or five half-grown little rabbits playing about her; one black and the others brown.

Cottontail had seen Tommy Brock passing in the distance. Asked whether her husband was at home she replied that Tommy Brock had rested twice while she watched him.

He had nodded, and pointed to the sack, and seemed doubled up with laughing.—"Come away,

Peter; he will be cooking them; come quicker!" said Benjamin Bunny.

They climbed up and up;—"He was at home; I saw his black ears peeping out of the hole." "They live too near the rocks to quarrel with their neighbors. Come on, Cousin Benjamin!"

When they came near the wood at the top of Bull Banks, they went cautiously. The trees grew amongst heaped up rocks; and there, beneath a crag, Mr. Tod had made one of his homes. It was at the top of a steep bank; the rocks and bushes overhung it. The rabbits crept up carefully, listening and peeping.

This house was something between a cave, a prison, and a tumbledown pigsty. There was a strong door, which was shut and locked.

The setting sun made the window panes glow like red flame; but the kitchen fire was not alight. It was neatly laid with dry sticks, as the rabbits could see, when they peeped through the window.

Benjamin sighed with relief.

But there were preparations upon the kitchen table which made him shudder. There was an immense empty pie dish of blue willow pattern, and a large carving knife and fork, and a chopper.

At the other end of the table was a partly unfolded tablecloth, a plate, a tumbler, a knife and fork, salt cellar, mustard and a chair—in short, preparations for one person's supper.

No person was to be seen, and no young rabbits. The kitchen was empty and silent; the clock had run down. Peter and Benjamin flattened their noses against the window, and stared into the dusk.

Then they scrambled round the rocks to the other side of the house. It was damp and smelly, and overgrown with thorns and briars.

The rabbits shivered in their shoes.

"Oh my poor rabbit babies! What a dreadful place; I shall never see them again!" sighed Benjamin.

They crept up to the bedroom window. It was closed and bolted like the kitchen. But there were signs that this window had been recently open; the cobwebs were disturbed, and there were fresh dirty footmarks upon the windowsill.

The room inside was so dark that at first they could make out nothing; but they could hear a noise—a slow deep regular snoring grunt. And as their eyes became accustomed to the darkness, they perceived that somebody was asleep on Mr. Tod's bed, curled up under the blanket.—"He has gone to bed in his boots," whispered Peter.

Benjamin, who was all of atwitter, pulled Peter off the windowsill.

Tommy Brock's snores continued, grunty and regular from Mr. Tod's bed. Nothing could be seen of the young family.

The sun had set; an owl began to hoot in the wood. There were many unpleasant things lying about that had much better have been buried; rabbit bones and skulls, and chickens' legs and other horrors. It was a shocking place, and very dark.

They went back to the front of the house, and tried in every way to move the bolt of the kitchen window. They tried to push up a rusty nail between the window sashes; but it was of no use, especially without a light.

They sat side by side outside the window, whispering and listening.

In half an hour the moon rose over the wood. It shone full and clear and cold, upon the house, amongst the rocks, and in at the kitchen window. But alas, no little rabbit babies were to be seen! The moonbeams twinkled on the carving knife and the pie dish, and

made a path of brightness across the dirty floor.

The light showed a little door in a wall beside the kitchen fireplace —a little iron door belonging to a brick oven of that old-fashioned sort that used to be heated with faggots of wood.

And presently at the same moment Peter and Benjamin noticed that whenever they shook the window the little door opposite shook in answer. The young family were alive; shut up in the oven!

Benjamin was so excited that it was a mercy he did not awake Tommy Brock, whose snores continued solemnly in Mr. Tod's bed.

But there really was not very much comfort in the discovery. They could not open the window; and although the young family was alive the little rabbits were quite incapable of letting themselves out; they were not old enough to crawl.

After much whispering, Peter and Benjamin decided to dig a tunnel. They began to burrow a yard or two lower down the bank. They hoped that they might be able to work between the large stones under the house; the kitchen floor was so dirty that it was impossible to say whether it was made of earth or flags.

They dug and dug for hours. They could not tunnel straight on account of stones; but by the end of the night they were under the kitchen floor. Benjamin was on his back scratching upwards. Peter's claws were worn down; he was outside the tunnel, shuffling sand away. He called out that it was morning—sunrise; and that the jays were making a noise down below in the woods.

Benjamin Bunny came out of the dark tunnel shaking the sand from his ears; he cleaned his face with his paws. Every minute the sun shone warmer on the top of the hill. In the valley there was a sea of white mist, with golden tops of trees showing through.

Again from the fields down below in the mist there came the angry cry of a jay, followed by the sharp yelping bark of a fox!

Then those two rabbits lost their heads completely. They did the most foolish thing that they could have done. They rushed into their short new tunnel, and hid themselves at the top end of it, under Mr. Tod's kitchen floor.

Mr. Tod was coming up Bull Banks, and he was in the very worst of tempers. First he had been upset by breaking the plate. It was his own fault; but it was a china plate, the last of the dinner service that had belonged to his grandmother, old Vixen Tod. Then the midges had been very bad. And he had failed to catch a hen pheasant on her nest; and it had contained only five eggs, two of them addled. Mr. Tod had had an unsatisfactory night.

As usual, when out of humor, he determined to move house. First he tried the pollard willow, but it was damp; and the otters had left a dead fish near it. Mr. Tod likes nobody's leavings but his own.

He made his way up the hill; his temper was not improved by notic-

ing unmistakable marks of badger. No one else grubs up the moss so wantonly as Tommy Brock.

Mr. Tod slapped his stick upon the earth and fumed; he guessed where Tommy Brock had gone to. He was further annoyed by the jay bird which followed him persistently. It flew from tree to tree and scolded, warning every rabbit within hearing that either a cat or a fox was coming up the plantation. Once when it flew screaming over his head Mr. Tod snapped at it, and barked.

He approached his house very carefully, with a large rusty key. He sniffed and his whiskers bristled.

The house was locked up, but Mr. Tod had his doubts whether it was empty. He turned the rusty key in the lock; the rabbits below could hear it. Mr. Tod opened the door cautiously and went in.

The sight that met Mr. Tod's eyes in Mr. Tod's kitchen made Mr. Tod furious. There was Mr. Tod's chair, and Mr. Tod's pie dish, and his knife and fork and mustard and salt cellar, and his tablecloth, that he had left folded up in the dresser —all set out for supper (or breakfast)—without doubt for that odious Tommy Brock.

There was a smell of fresh earth and dirty badger, which fortunately overpowered all smell of rabbit.

But what absorbed Mr. Tod's attention was a noise, a deep slow regular snoring grunting noise, coming from his own bed.

He peeped through the hinges of the half-open bedroom door. Then he turned and came out of the house in a hurry. His whiskers bristled and his coat collar stood on end with rage.

For the next twenty minutes Mr. Tod kept creeping cautiously into the house, and retreating hurriedly out again. By degrees he ventured further in—right into the bedroom. When he was outside the house, he scratched up the earth with fury. But when he was inside —he did not like the look of Tommy Brock's teeth.

He was lying on his back with his mouth open, grinning from ear to ear. He snored peacefully and regularly; but one eye was not perfectly shut.

Mr. Tod came in and out of the bedroom. Twice he brought in his walking stick, and once he brought culiar, and rather difficult (because the bed was between the window and the door of the bedroom). He opened the window a little way, and pushed out the greater part of the clothes line on to the window-sill. The rest of the line, with a hook at the end, remained in his hand.

Tommy Brock snored conscientiously. Mr. Tod stood and looked at him for a minute; then he left the room again.

in the coal scuttle. But he thought better of it, and took them away.

When he came back after removing the coal scuttle, Tommy Brock was lying a little more sideways; but he seemed even sounder asleep. He was an incurably indolent person; he was not in the least afraid of Mr. Tod; he was simply too lazy and comfortable to move.

Mr. Tod came back yet again into the bedroom with a clothes line. He stood a minute watching Tommy Brock and listening attentively to the snores. They were very loud indeed, but seemed quite natural.

Mr. Tod turned his back towards the bed, and undid the window. It creaked; he turned round with a jump. Tommy Brock, who had opened one eye—shut it hastily. The snores continued.

Mr. Tod's proceedings were pe-

Tommy Brock opened both eyes, and looked at the rope and grinned. There was a noise outside the window. Tommy Brock shut his eyes in a hurry.

Mr. Tod had gone out at the front door, and round to the back of the house. On the way, he stumbled over the rabbit burrow. If he had had any idea who was inside it he would have pulled them out quickly.

His foot went through the tunnel nearly upon the top of Peter Rabbit and Benjamin; but, fortunately, he

Mr. Tod put down the pail beside the bed, took up the end of rope with the hook—hesitated, and looked at Tommy Brock. The snores were almost apoplectic; but the grin was not quite so big.

Mr. Tod gingerly mounted a chair by the head of the bedstead. His legs were dangerously near to Tommy Brock's teeth.

He reached up and put the end of rope, with the hook, over the head of the tester bed, where the curtains ought to hang.

thought that it was some more of Tommy Brock's work.

He took up the coil of line from the sill, listened for a moment, and then tied the rope to a tree.

Tommy Brock watched him with one eye, through the window. He was puzzled.

Mr. Tod fetched a large heavy pailful of water from the spring, and staggered with it through the kitchen into his bedroom.

Tommy Brock snored industriously, with rather a snort.

(Mr. Tod's curtains were folded up, and put away, owing to the house being unoccupied. So was the counterpane. Tommy Brock was covered with a blanket only.) Mr. Tod standing on the unsteady chair looked down upon him attentively; he really was a first prize sound sleeper!

It seemed as though nothing would waken him—not even the flapping rope across the bed.

Mr. Tod descended safely from the chair, and endeavored to get up again with the pail of water. He intended to hang it from the hook, dangling over the head of Tommy Brock, in order to make a sort of shower-bath, worked by a string, through the window.

But, naturally, being a thin-legged person (though vindictive and sandy whiskered)—he was quite unable to lift the heavy weight to the level of the hook and rope. He very nearly overbalanced himself.

The snores became more and more apoplectic. One of Tommy Brock's hind legs twitched under the blanket, but still he slept on peacefully.

Mr. Tod and the pail descended from the chair without accident. After considerable thought, he emptied the water into a wash basin and jug. The empty pail was not too heavy for him; he slung it up wobbling over the head of Tommy Brock.

Surely there never was such a sleeper! Mr. Tod got up and down, down and up on the chair.

As he could not lift the whole pailful of water at once he fetched a milk jug and ladled quarts of water into the pail by degrees. The pail got fuller and fuller, and swung like a pendulum. Occasionally a drop splashed over; but still Tommy Brock snored regularly and never moved,—except in one eye.

At last Mr. Tod's preparations were complete. The pail was full of water; the rope was tightly strained over the top of the bed, and across the windowsill to the tree outside.

"It will make a great mess in my bedroom; but I could never sleep in that bed again without a spring cleaning of some sort," said Mr. Tod.

Mr. Tod took a last look at the badger and softly left the room. He went out of the house, shutting the front door. The rabbits heard his footsteps over the tunnel.

He ran round behind the house, intending to undo the rope in order to let fall the pailful of water upon Tommy Brock—

"I will wake him up with an unpleasant surprise," said Mr. Tod.

The moment he had gone, Tommy Brock got up in a hurry; he rolled Mr. Tod's dressing-gown into a bundle, put it into the bed beneath the pail of water instead of himself, and left the room also—grinning immensely.

He went into the kitchen, lighted the fire and boiled the kettle; for the moment he did not trouble himself to cook the baby rabbits.

and quite knocked him over backwards.

Inside the house there was a great crash and splash, and the noise of a pail rolling over and over.

But no screams. Mr. Tod was mystified; he sat quite still, and listened attentively. Then he peeped in at the window. The water was dripping from the bed, the pail had rolled into a corner.

In the middle of the bed, under the blanket, was a wet *something* —much flattened in the middle, where the pail had caught it (as it were across the tummy). Its head was covered by the wet blanket, and it was *not snoring any longer*.

When Mr. Tod got to the tree, he found that the weight and strain had dragged the knot so tight that it was past untying. He was obliged to gnaw it with his teeth. He chewed and gnawed for more than twenty minutes. At last the rope gave way with such a sudden jerk that it nearly pulled his teeth out,

There was nothing stirring, and no sound except the drip, drop, drop, drip, of water trickling from the mattress.

Mr. Tod watched it for half an hour; his eyes glistened.

Then he cut a caper, and became so bold that he even tapped at the window; but the bundle never moved.

Yes—there was no doubt about it—it had turned out even better than he had planned; the pail had hit poor old Tommy Brock, and killed him dead!

"I will bury that nasty person in the hole which he has dug. I will bring my bedding out, and dry it in the sun," said Mr. Tod.

"I will wash the tablecloth and spread it on the grass in the sun to bleach. And the blanket must be hung up in the wind; and the bed must be thoroughly disinfected, and aired with a warming-pan; and warmed with a hot water bottle."

"I will get soft soap, and monkey soap, and all sorts of soap; and soda and scrubbing brushes; and persian powder; and carbolic to remove the smell. I must have a disinfecting. Perhaps I may have to burn sulphur."

He hurried round the house to get a shovel from the kitchen—"First I will arrange the hole—then I will drag out that person in the blanket. . . ."

He opened the door. . . .

Tommy Brock was sitting at Mr. Tod's kitchen table, pouring out tea from Mr. Tod's teapot into Mr. Tod's teacup. He was quite dry himself and grinning; and he threw the cup of scalding tea all over Mr. Tod.

Then Mr. Tod rushed upon Tommy Brock, and Tommy Brock grappled with Mr. Tod amongst the broken crockery, and there was a terrific battle all over the kitchen. To the rabbits underneath it sounded as if the floor would give way at each crash of falling furniture.

oven woke up trembling; perhaps it was fortunate they were shut up inside.

They crept out of their tunnel, and hung about amongst the rocks and bushes, listening anxiously.

Everything was upset except the kitchen table.

And everything was broken, except the mantelpiece and the kitchen fender. The crockery was smashed to atoms.

The chairs were broken, and the window, and the clock fell with a crash, and there were handfuls of Mr. Tod's sandy whiskers.

The vases fell off the mantelpiece, the cannisters fell off the shelf; the kettle fell off the hob. Tommy Brock put his foot in a jar of raspberry jam.

Inside the house the racket was fearful. The rabbit babies in the

And the boiling water out of the kettle fell upon the tail of Mr. Tod.

When the kettle fell, Tommy Brock, who was still grinning, happened to be uppermost; and he rolled Mr. Tod over and over like a log, out at the door.

Then the snarling and worrying went on outside; and they rolled over the bank, and down hill, bumping over the rocks. There will never be any love lost between Tommy Brock and Mr. Tod.

As soon as the coast was clear, Peter Rabbit and Benjamin Bunny came out of the bushes.

"Now for it! Run in, Cousin Benjamin! Run in and get them! while I watch the door."

But Benjamin was frightened—

"Oh; oh! they are coming back!"

"No they are not."

"Yes they are!"

"What dreadful bad language! I think they have fallen down the stone quarry."

Still Benjamin hesitated, and Peter kept pushing him—

"Be quick, it's all right. Shut the oven door, Cousin Benjamin, so that he won't miss them."

Decidedly there were lively doings in Mr. Tod's kitchen!

At home in the rabbit hole, things had not been quite comfortable.

After quarreling at supper, Flopsy and old Mr. Bouncer had passed a sleepless night, and quarrelled again at breakfast. Old Mr. Bouncer could no longer deny that he had invited company into the rabbit hole; but he refused to reply to the questions and reproaches of Flopsy. The day passed heavily.

Old Mr. Bouncer, very sulky, was huddled up in a corner, barricaded with a chair. Flopsy had taken and found something warm and wriggling. He lifted it out carefully, and rejoined Peter Rabbit.

"I've got them! Can we get away? Shall we hide, Cousin Peter?"

Peter pricked his ears; distant sounds of fighting still echoed in the wood.

Five minutes afterwards two breathless rabbits came scuttering away down Bull Banks, half carrying, half dragging a sack between them, bumpetty bump over the grass. They reached home safely, and burst into the rabbit hole.

away his pipe and hidden the tobacco. She had been having a complete turn out and spring cleaning, to relieve her feelings. She had just finished. Old Mr. Bouncer, behind his chair, was wondering anxiously what she would do next.

In Mr. Tod's kitchen, amidst the wreckage, Benjamin Bunny picked his way to the oven nervously, through a thick cloud of dust. He opened the oven door, felt inside,

Great was old Mr. Bouncer's relief and Flopsy's joy when Peter and Benjamin arrived in triumph with

the young family. The rabbit babies were rather tumbled and very hungry; they were fed and put to bed. They soon recovered.

A new long pipe and a fresh supply of rabbit tobacco was presented to Mr. Bouncer. He was rather upon his dignity; but he accepted.

Old Mr. Bouncer was forgiven, and they all had dinner. Then Peter and Benjamin told their story—but they had not waited long enough to be able to tell the end of the battle

between Tommy Brock and Mr. Tod.

THE TALE OF
PIGLING
BLAND

For Cecily and Charlie,
a Tale of the Christmas Pig

Once upon a time there was an old pig called Aunt Pettitoes. She had eight of a family: four little girl pigs, called Cross-patch, Suck-suck, Yock-yock and Spot; and four little boy pigs, called Alexander, Pigling Bland, Chin-Chin and Stumpy. Stumpy had had an accident to his tail.

The eight little pigs had very fine appetites—"Yus, yus, yus! they eat and indeed they *do* eat!" said Aunt Pettitoes, looking at her family with pride. Suddenly there were fearful squeals; Alexander had squeezed inside the hoops of the pig trough and stuck.

Aunt Pettitoes and I dragged him out by the hind legs.

Chin-chin was already in disgrace; it was washing day, and he had eaten a piece of soap. And presently in a basket of clean clothes, we found another dirty little pig—"Tchut, tut, tut! whichever is this?" grunted Aunt Pettitoes.

Now all the pig family are pink, or pink with black spots, but this pig child was smutty black all over; when it had been popped into a tub, it proved to be Yock-yock.

I went into the garden; there I found Cross-patch and Suck-suck rooting up carrots. I whipped them myself and led them out by the ears. Cross-patch tried to bite me.

"Aunt Pettitoes, Aunt Pettitoes! you are a worthy person, but your family is not well brought up. Every one of them has been in mischief except Spot and Pigling Bland."

"Yus, yus!" sighed Aunt Pettitoes. "And they drink bucketfuls of milk; I shall have to get another cow! Good little Spot shall stay at home to do the housework; but the others must go. Four little boy pigs and four little girl pigs are too many altogether." "Yus, yus, yus," said Aunt Pettitoes, "there will be more to eat without them."

So Chin-chin and Suck-suck went

away in a wheel-barrow, and Stumpy, Yock-yock and Cross-patch rode away in a cart.

And the other two little boy pigs, Pigling Bland and Alexander went to market. We brushed their coats, we curled their tails and washed their little faces, and wished them good bye in the yard.

Aunt Pettitoes wiped her eyes

with a large pocket handkerchief, then she wiped Pigling Bland's nose and shed tears; then she wiped Alexander's nose and shed tears; then she passed the handkerchief to Spot. Aunt Pettitoes sighed and grunted, and addressed those little pigs as follows—

"Now Pigling Bland, son Pigling Bland, you must go to market. Take your brother Alexander by the hand. Mind your Sunday clothes, and remember to blow your nose" —(Aunt Pettitoes passed round the handkerchief again)—"beware of traps, hen roosts, bacon and eggs; always walk upon your hind legs." Pigling Bland who was a sedate little pig, looked solemnly at his mother, a tear trickled down his cheek.

Aunt Pettitoes turned to the other—"Now son Alexander take the hand"—"Wee, wee, wee!" giggled Alexander—"take the hand of your brother Pigling Bland, you must go to market. Mind—" "Wee, wee, wee!" interrupted Alexander again. "You put me out," said Aunt Pettitoes—"Observe signposts and milestones; do not gobble herring bones—" "And remember," said I impressively, "if you once cross the county boundary you cannot come back. Alexander, you are not at-

tending. Here are two licenses permitting two pigs to go to market in Lancashire. Attend Alexander. I have had no end of trouble in getting these papers from the policeman." Pigling Bland listened gravely; Alexander was hopelessly volatile.

I pinned the papers, for safety, inside their waistcoat pockets; Aunt Pettitoes gave to each a little bundle, and eight conversation peppermints with appropriate moral sentiments in screws of paper. Then they started.

Pigling Bland and Alexander trotted along steadily for a mile; at least Pigling Bland did. Alexander made the road half as long again by skipping from side to side. He danced about and pinched his brother, singing—

"This pig went to market, this pig stayed
    at home,
"This pig had a bit of meat—

let's see what they have given *us* for dinner, Pigling?"

Pigling Bland and Alexander sat down and untied their bundles. Alexander gobbled up his dinner in no time; he had already eaten all his own peppermints—"Give me one of yours, please, Pigling?" "But I wish to preserve them for emergencies," said Pigling Bland doubtfully. Alexander went into squeals of laughter. Then he pricked Pigling with the pin that had fastened his pig paper; and when Pigling slapped him he dropped the pin, and tried to take Pigling's pin, and the papers got mixed up. Pigling Bland reproved Alexander.

But presently they made it up again, and trotted away together, singing—

"Tom, Tom the piper's son, stole a pig
    and away he ran!
"But all the tune that he could play, was
    'Over the hills and far away!' "

"What's that, young Sirs? Stole a pig? Where are your licenses?" said the policeman. They had nearly run against him round a corner. Pigling Bland pulled out his paper; Alexander, after fumbling, handed over something scrumply—

"To 2½ oz. conversation sweeties at three farthings"—"What's this? this ain't a license?" Alexander's nose lengthened visibly, he had lost it. "I had one, indeed I had, Mr. Policeman!"

time, followed by a damp subdued little pig. I disposed of Alexander in the neighborhood; he did fairly well when he had settled down.

"It's not likely they let you start without. I am passing the farm. You may walk with me." "Can I come back too?" inquired Pigling Bland. "I see no reason, young Sir; your paper is all right." Pigling Bland did not like going on alone, and it was beginning to rain. But it is unwise to argue with the police; he gave his brother a peppermint, and watched him out of sight.

Pigling Bland went on alone dejectedly; he came to cross roads and a sign-post—"To Market-town 5 miles," "Over the Hills, 4 miles," "To Pettitoes Farm, 3 miles."

To conclude the adventures of Alexander—the policeman sauntered up to the house about tea

Pigling Bland was shocked, there was little hope of sleeping in Market Town, and tomorrow was the hiring fair; it was deplorable to think how much time had been wasted by the frivolity of Alexander.

He glanced wistfully along the road towards the hills, and then set off walking obediently the other way, buttoning up his coat against the rain. He had never wanted to go; and the idea of standing all by himself in a crowded market, to be stared at, pushed, and hired by some big strange farmer was very disagreeable—

"I wish I could have a little garden and grow potatoes," said Pigling Bland.

He put his cold hand in his pocket and felt his paper, he put his other hand in his other pocket and felt another paper—Alexander's! Pigling squealed; then ran back frantically, hoping to overtake Alexander and the policeman.

He took a wrong turn—several wrong turns, and was quite lost.

It grew dark, the wind whistled, the trees creaked and groaned.

Pigling Bland became frightened and cried "Wee, wee, wee! I can't find my way home!"

After an hour's wandering he got out of the wood; the moon shone through the clouds, and Pigling Bland saw a country that was new to him.

The road crossed a moor; below was a wide valley with a river twinkling in the moonlight, and beyond —in misty distance—lay the hills.

He saw a small wooden hut, made his way to it, and crept inside —"I am afraid it *is* a hen house, but what can I do?" said Pigling Bland, wet and cold and quite tired out.

"Bacon and eggs, bacon and eggs!" clucked a hen on a perch.

"Trap, trap, trap! cackle, cackle, cackle!" scolded the disturbed cockerel. "To market, to market! jiggetty jig!" clucked a broody white hen roosting next to him. Pigling Bland, much alarmed, determined to leave at daybreak. In the meantime, he and the hens fell asleep.

In less than an hour they were all awakened. The owner, Mr. Peter Thomas Piperson, came with a lantern and a hamper to catch six fowls to take to market in the morning.

He grabbed the white hen roosting next to the cock; then his eye fell upon Pigling Bland, squeezed up in a corner. He made a singular remark—"Hallo, here's another!" —seized Pigling by the scruff of the neck, and dropped him into the hamper. Then he dropped in five more dirty, kicking, cackling hens upon the top of Pigling Bland.

The hamper containing six fowls and a young pig was no light weight; it was taken down hill, unsteadily, with jerks. Pigling, although nearly scratched to pieces, contrived to hide the papers and peppermints inside his clothes.

At last the hamper was bumped

down upon a kitchen floor, the lid was opened, and Pigling was lifted out. He looked up, blinking, and saw an offensively ugly elderly man, grinning from ear to ear.

"This one's come of himself, whatever," said Mr. Piperson, turning Pigling's pockets inside out. He pushed the hamper into a corner, threw a sack over it to keep the hens quiet, put a pot on the fire, and unlaced his boots.

Pigling Bland drew forward a coppy stool, and sat on the edge of it, shyly warming his hands. Mr. Piperson pulled off a boot and threw it against the wainscot at the further end of the kitchen. There was a smothered noise—"Shut up!" said Mr. Piperson. Pigling Bland warmed his hands, and eyed him.

Mr. Piperson pulled off the other boot and flung it after the first, there was again a curious noise— "Be quiet, will ye?" said Mr. Piper-

son. Pigling Bland sat on the very edge of the coppy stool.

Mr. Piperson fetched meal from a chest and made porridge, it seemed to Pigling that something at the further end of the kitchen was taking a suppressed interest in the cooking; but he was too hungry to be troubled by noises.

Mr. Piperson poured out three platefuls: for himself, for Pigling, and a third—after glaring at Pigling—he put away with much scuffling, and locked up. Pigling Bland ate his supper discreetly.

After supper Mr. Piperson consulted an almanac, and felt Pigling's ribs; it was too late in the season for curing bacon, and he grudged his meal. Besides, the hens had seen this pig.

He looked at the small remains of a flitch [side of bacon], and then looked undecidedly at Pigling. "You

It crossed Pigling's mind that if *he* had asked for a lift, too, he might still have been in time for market.

may sleep on the rug," said Mr. Peter Thomas Piperson.

Pigling Bland slept like a top. In the morning Mr. Piperson made more porridge; the weather was warmer. He looked how much meal was left in the chest, and seemed dissatisfied—"You'll likely be moving on again?" said he to Pigling Bland.

Before Pigling could reply, a neighbor, who was giving Mr. Piperson and the hens a lift, whistled from the gate. Mr. Piperson hurried out with the hamper, enjoining Pigling to shut the door behind him and not meddle with nought; or "I'll come back and skin ye!" said Mr. Piperson.

But he distrusted Peter Thomas.

After finishing breakfast at his leisure, Pigling had a look round the cottage; everything was locked up. He found some potato peelings in a bucket in the back kitchen. Pigling ate the peel, and washed up the porridge plates in the bucket. He sang while he worked—

"Tom with his pipe made such a noise,
  He called up all the girls and boys—
"And they all ran to hear him play,
  "Over the hills and far away!—"

Suddenly a little smothered voice chimed in—

"Over the hills and a great way off,
  The wind shall blow my top knot off!"

cupboard, and snuffed at the key-hole. It was quite quiet.

Pigling Bland put down a plate which he was wiping, and listened.

After a long pause, Pigling went on tiptoe and peeped round the door into the front kitchen; there was nobody there.

After another pause, Pigling approached the door of the locked

After another long pause, Pigling pushed a peppermint under the door. It was sucked in immediately.

In the course of the day Pigling pushed in all his remaining six peppermints.

When Mr. Piperson returned, he found Pigling sitting before the fire; he had brushed up the hearth and put on the pot to boil; the meal was not get-at-able.

Mr. Piperson was very affable; he slapped Pigling on the back, made lots of porridge and forgot to lock the meal chest. He did lock the cupboard door; but without properly shutting it. He went to bed early, and told Pigling upon no account to disturb him next day before twelve o'clock.

Pigling Bland sat by the fire, eating his supper.

All at once at his elbow, a little voice spoke—"My name is Pig-wig. Make me more porridge, please!" Pigling Bland jumped, and looked round.

A perfectly lovely little black Berkshire pig stood smiling beside him. She had twinkly little screwed up eyes, a double chin, and a short turned up nose.

She pointed at Pigling's plate; he hastily gave it to her, and fled to the meal chest—"How did you come here?" asked Pigling Bland.

"Stolen," replied Pig-wig, with her mouth full. Pigling helped himself to meal without scruple. "What for?" "Bacon, hams," replied Pig-wig cheerfully. "Why on earth don't you run away?" exclaimed the horrified Pigling.

"I shall after supper," said Pig-wig decidedly.

Pigling Bland made more porridge and watched her shyly.

She finished a second plate, got up, and looked about her, as though she were going to start.

"You can't go in the dark," said Pigling Bland.

Pig-wig looked anxious.

"Do you know your way by daylight?"

"I know we can see this little white house from the hills across the river. Which way are *you* going, Mr. Pig?"

"To market—I have two pig papers. I might take you to the bridge; if you have no objection," said

Pigling much confused and sitting on the edge of his coppy stool. Pig-wig's gratitude was such and she asked so many questions that it became embarrassing to Pigling Bland.

He was obliged to shut his eyes and pretend to sleep. She became quiet, and there was a smell of peppermint.

"I thought you had eaten them?" said Pigling, waking suddenly.

"Only the corners," replied Pig-wig, studying the sentiments with much interest by the firelight.

"I wish you wouldn't; he might smell them through the ceiling," said the alarmed Pigling.

Pig-wig put back the sticky peppermints into her pocket; "Sing something," she demanded.

"I am sorry . . . I have toothache," said Pigling much dismayed.

"Then I will sing," replied Pig-wig, "You will not mind if I say iddy tidditty? I have forgotten some of the words."

Pigling Bland made no objection; he sat with his eyes half shut, and watched her.

She wagged her head and rocked about, clapping time and singing in a sweet little grunty voice—

"A funny old mother pig lived in a stye,
    and three little piggies had she;
"(Ti idditty idditty) umph, umph,
    umph! and the little pigs said wee,
    wee!"

She sang successfully through three or four verses, only at every verse her head nodded a little lower, and her little twinkly eyes closed up—

"Those three little piggies grew peaky and lean, and lean they might very well be;
"For somehow they couldn't say umph, umph, umph! and they wouldn't say wee, wee, wee!
"For somehow they couldn't say—

Pig-wig's head bobbed lower and lower, until she rolled over, a little round ball, fast asleep on the hearth-rug.

Pigling Bland, on tiptoe, covered her up with an antimacassar.

He was afraid to go to sleep himself; for the rest of the night he sat listening to the chirping of the crickets and to the snores of Mr. Piperson overhead.

Early in the morning, between dark and daylight, Pigling tied up his little bundle and woke up Pig-wig. She was excited and half-frightened. "But it's dark! How can we find our way?"

"The cock has crowed; we must start before the hens come out; they might shout to Mr. Piperson."

Pig-wig sat down again, and commenced to cry.

"Come away Pig-wig; we can see when we get used to it. Come! I can hear them clucking!"

Pigling had never said shuh! to a hen in his life, being peaceable; also he remembered the hamper.

He opened the house door quietly and shut it after them. There was no garden; the neighborhood of Mr. Piperson's was all scratched up by fowls. They slipped away hand in hand across an untidy field to the road.

"Tom, Tom the piper's son, stole a pig
    and away he ran!
"But all the tune that he could play, was
    'Over the hills and far away!' "

"Come Pig-wig, we must get to the bridge before folks are stirring."

"Why do you want to go to market, Pigling?" inquired Pig-wig

The sun rose while they were crossing the moor, a dazzle of light over the tops of the hills. The sunshine crept down the slopes into the peaceful green valleys, where little white cottages nestled in gardens and orchards.

"That's Westmorland," said Pig-wig. She dropped Pigling's hand and commenced to dance, sing-ing—

presently. "I don't want; I want to grow potatoes." "Have a peppermint?" said Pig-wig. Pigling Bland refused quite crossly. "Does your poor toothy hurt?" inquired Pig-wig. Pigling Bland grunted.

Pig-wig ate the peppermint herself, and followed the opposite side of the road. "Pig-wig! keep under the wall, there's a man ploughing." Pig-wig crossed over, they hurried down hill towards the county boundary.

Suddenly Pigling stopped; he heard wheels.

Slowly jogging up the road below them came a tradesman's cart. The reins flapped on the horse's back, the grocer was reading a newspaper.

"Take that peppermint out of your mouth, Pig-wig, we may have to run. Don't say one word. Leave it to me. And in sight of the bridge!" said poor Pigling, nearly crying. He began to walk frightfully lame, holding Pig-wig's arm.

The grocer, intent upon his newspaper, might have passed them, if his horse had not shied and snorted. He pulled the cart crossways, and held down his whip. "Hallo? Where are *you* going to?"—Pigling Bland stared at him vacantly.

"Are you deaf? Are you going to market?" Pigling nodded slowly.

"I thought as much. It was yesterday. Show me your license?"

Pigling stared at the off hind shoe of the grocer's horse which had picked up a stone.

The grocer flicked his whip— "Papers? Pig license?" Pigling fumbled in all his pockets, and handed up the papers. The grocer read them, but still seemed dissatisfied. "This here pig is a young lady; is her name Alexander?" Pig-wig opened her mouth and shut it again; Pigling coughed asthmatically.

The grocer ran his finger down the advertisement column of his newspaper—"Lost, stolen or strayed, 10s. reward;" he looked suspiciously at Pig-wig. Then he stood up in the trap, and whistled for the ploughman.

"You wait here while I drive on and speak to him," said the grocer, gathering up the reins. He knew that pigs are slippery; but surely, such a *very* lame pig could never run!

"Not yet, Pig-wig, he will look back." The grocer did so; he saw the two pigs stock-still in the middle of the road. Then he looked over at his horse's heels; it was lame also; the stone took some time to knock out, after he got to the ploughman.

"Now, Pig-wig, NOW!" said Pigling Bland.

Never did any pigs run as these pigs ran! They raced and squealed

and pelted down the long white hill towards the bridge. Little fat Pig-wig's petticoats fluttered, and her feet went pitter, patter, pitter, as she bounded and jumped.

They ran, and they ran, and they ran down the hill, and across a short cut on level green turf at the bottom, between pebble beds and rushes.

They came to the river, they came to the bridge—they crossed it hand in hand—then over the hills and far away she danced with Pigling Bland!

GINGER AND PICKLES

Dedicated
With very kind regards to old Mr. John Taylor,
Who "thinks he might pass as a dormouse,"
(Three years in bed and never a grumble!).

Once upon a time there was a village shop. The name over the window was "Ginger and Pickles."

It was a little small shop just the right size for Dolls—Lucinda and Jane Doll-cook always bought their groceries at Ginger and Pickles.

The counter inside was a convenient height for rabbits. Ginger and Pickles sold red spotty pocket handkerchiefs at a penny three farthings.

They also sold sugar, and snuff and galoshes.

In fact, although it was such a small shop it sold nearly everything—except a few things that you want in a hurry—like bootlaces, hairpins and mutton chops.

Ginger and Pickles were the people who kept the shop. Ginger was a yellow tomcat, and Pickles was a terrier.

The rabbits were always a little bit afraid of Pickles.

The shop was also patronized by mice—only the mice were rather afraid of Ginger.

Ginger usually requested Pickles to serve them, because he said it made his mouth water.

"I cannot bear," said he, "to see them going out at the door carrying their little parcels."

"I have the same feeling about rats," replied Pickles, "but it would never do to eat our customers; they would leave us and go to Tabitha Twitchit's."

"On the contrary, they would go nowhere," replied Ginger gloomily.

(Tabitha Twitchit kept the only other shop in the village. She did not give credit.)

Ginger and Pickles gave unlimited credit.

Now the meaning of "credit" is this—when a customer buys a bar of soap, instead of the customer pulling out a purse and paying for it —she says she will pay another time.

And Pickles makes a low bow and says, "With pleasure, madam," and it is written down in a book.

The customers come again and again, and buy quantities, in spite of being afraid of Ginger and Pickles.

But there is no money in what is called the "till."

The customers came in crowds every day and bought quantities, especially the toffee customers. But there was always no money; they never paid for as much as a pennyworth of peppermints.

But the sales were enormous, ten times as large as Tabitha Twitchit's.

As there was always no money, Ginger and Pickles were obliged to eat their own goods.

Pickles ate biscuits and Ginger ate a dried haddock.

They ate them by candle-light after the shop was closed.

When it came to Jan. ɪst there was still no money, and Pickles was unable to buy a dog license.

"It is very unpleasant, I am afraid of the police," said Pickles.

"It is your own fault for being a terrier; *I* do not require a license, and neither does Kep, the Collie dog."

"It is very uncomfortable, I am afraid I shall be summoned. I have tried in vain to get a license upon credit at the Post Office;" said Pickles. "The place is full of policemen. I met one as I was coming home.

"Let us send in the bill again to Samuel Whiskers, Ginger, he owes 22/9 for bacon."

"I do not believe that he intends to pay at all," replied Ginger.

"And I feel sure that Anna Maria pockets things—

"Where are all the cream crackers?"

"You have eaten them yourself," replied Ginger.

Ginger and Pickles retired into the back parlor.

They did accounts. They added up sums and sums, and sums.

"Samuel Whiskers has run up a bill as long as his tail; he has had an ounce and three-quarters of snuff since October.

"What is seven pounds of butter at 1/3, and a stick of sealing wax and four matches?"

"Send in all the bills again to everybody 'with compliments,' " replied Ginger.

After a time they heard a noise in the shop, as if something had been pushed in at the door. They came out of the back parlor. There was an envelope lying on the counter, and a policeman writing in a notebook!

Pickles nearly had a fit, he barked and he barked and made little rushes.

"Bite him, Pickles! bite him!" spluttered Ginger behind a sugar barrel, "he's only a German doll!"

The policeman went on writing in his notebook; twice he put his pencil in his mouth, and once he dipped it in the treacle.

Pickles barked till he was hoarse. But still the policeman took no notice. He had bead eyes, and his helmet was sewed on with stitches.

At length on his last little rush—Pickles found that the shop was empty. The policeman had disappeared.

But the envelope remained.

"Do you think that he has gone to fetch a real live policeman? I am afraid it is a summons," said Pickles.

"No," replied Ginger, who had opened the envelope, "it is the rates and taxes, £3 19 11¾."

"This is the last straw," said Pickles, "let us close the shop."

They put up the shutters, and left. But they have not removed from the neighborhood. In fact some people wish they had gone further.

Ginger is living in the war-
ren [game preserve for rab-
bits]. I do not know what
occupation he pursues; he
looks stout and comfortable.

Pickles is at present a game-
keeper.

The closing of the shop caused great inconvenience. Tabitha Twitchit immediately raised the price of everything a halfpenny; and she continued to refuse to give credit.

Of course there are the tradesmen's carts—the butcher, the fishman and Timothy Baker.

But a person cannot live on "seed wigs" and sponge cake and butter buns—not even when the sponge cake is as good as Timothy's!

After a time Mr. John Dormouse and his daughter began to sell peppermints and candles.

But they did not keep "self-fitting sixes"; and it takes five mice to carry one seven inch candle.

Besides—the candles which they sell behave very strangely in warm weather.

And Miss Dormouse refused to take back the ends when they were brought back to her with complaints.

And when Mr. John Dormouse was complained to, he stayed in bed, and would say nothing but "very snug;" which is not the way to carry on a retail business.

So everybody was pleased when Sally Henny Penny sent out a printed poster to say that she was going to reopen the shop—"Henny's Opening Sale! Grand cooperative Jumble! Penny's penny prices! Come buy, come try, come buy!"

The poster really was most 'ticing.

There was a rush upon the opening day. The shop was crammed with customers, and there were crowds of mice upon the biscuit cannisters.

Sally Henny Penny gets rather flustered when she tries to count out change, and she insists on being paid cash; but she is quite harmless.

And she has laid in a remarkable assortment of bargains.

There is something to please everybody.